# GHOST IN THE PARK

### RAY MELNIK

iUniverse

# GHOST IN THE PARK

*The novel is set in Staten Island, New York, just across the ferry from Manhattan. Some locations mentioned such as Tompkinsville Park, Staten Island Ferry and other local landmarks, are real, some are not, but all the characters in the novella are fictitious. Any similarities to people in real life is purely accidental. Other landmarks and locations described in the novel are real.*

*iUniverse books may be ordered through booksellers or by contacting:*

*iUniverse*
*1663 Liberty Drive*
*Bloomington, IN 47403*
*www.iuniverse.com*
*1-800-Authors (1-800-288-4677)*

*ISBN: 978-1-4917-9570-5 (sc)*
*ISBN: 978-1-4917-9571-2 (e)*

*Print information available on the last page.*

*iUniverse rev. date: 4/29/2016*

Dedicated as hope for those for whom
love is still just a ghost.

# ACKNOWLEDGMENTS

*Special thanks to Angie Ruiz for editing.*

*Thanks to*
*Amanda Flowers – cover model*
*Kristopher Johnson – cover photographer*
*ntech media design – cover layout*
Elysium Eight for the video introduction
Sara, the inspiration for the character Amber
All the great folks at the Everything Goes Book Cafe

# PROLOGUE

All the greatest ideas to realize, or mysteries to be solved, are seeds born in the human mind. The wish to understand them is the gardener in each of us, but the only true path to their growth and successful harvest, is to start with a fertile soil.

Most of us have choices in life, and those who don't are the ones who need our help. Amber was a beautiful soul trapped in a young woman, abused as a child. She was riddled with anxiety, often depressed and she had no idea that life could be anything other than one filled with sadness. Then she met Sami. Only a special person can see the flower that grows from the ashes. Sami was that person, but his love was too much, too late. Or was it?

In the littlest park in a tiny corner of Staten Island, New York, realities will collide. Unintended consequences from events will alter lives. One to uncover a secret, another to confess, and the last to save a love.

Sami Bell took his thin jacket from the corner of the couch, wrapped his laptop strap around his shoulder and backed out the door before locking both deadbolts. It was a tepid day in mid-May, a little warmer than he had expected, which was immediately evident by the change in smell. It was that first sign, noticed by the senses, of life beginning to grow again. He tucked the jacket into his bag since it would only be needed for the breezy ride across the harbor. It was obvious it was milder during the night too, by his sense of sight, since the few homeless people in the area moved from sheltering in doorways to sleeping openly on the benches in Tompkinsville Park just outside his apartment door. The park was almost a block long, triangular in shape at the far end, with a large center area paved with six sided gray bricks. There were areas of grass and trees delineated by short green iron fencing and stretches of dark green colored chain and poles. The chain was possibly meant to signal keep off the grass, but that was never clear to the children in the area. None of the chained in areas had received early maintenance. There were scattered branches and blown leaves left from the winter.

It was a park overlooked by services, with many people fearing walking through it once the sun went down. As long as the sun was up, mothers would still bring their children to play, and others would enter. It was a rather strange mix of patrons. The homeless would make themselves scarce once the sun rose and the poorer locals from the area with nowhere to go, would line up on the stoops along the stores across from the park. There were even the occasional tourist couples that stumbled upon it in their explorative walks down from the ferry. While most in the neighborhood wished it were as friendly as when they celebrated St George Day, most knew that the area's lack of affluence relegated it to second class services.

It was a short walk for Sami on Bay Street past the luxury apartments near the water. Always early, there would be no chance of missing the 7:30 am ferry. Seeing these buildings was repeatedly a little annoying to Sami. It had been his and Amber's goal to move from their apartment to their own condo in one of those buildings. Those buildings had their own private roads, their own private park areas, away from everyone. The views of the harbor were the best on Staten Island, and it was because of those buildings that diverse stores began to open in the area. Sami was on track too. Only twenty-four years old, he had landed a respectable position in graphic design for a law firm in midtown. His work was exemplary and appreciated. It would just be a matter of time before he could afford the move. But none of that really mattered to him now.

Amber was a beautiful young girl, long layered blonde hair, and blue eyes that grabbed you and wouldn't let you go. But her beauty came with a bit of a troubled anxious side. She grew up in an abusive home, which she'd always accepted as normal. Once she was old enough to see the abuse for what it was, she decided to run away from it. When Sami met her, she had been staying with the owners of the 'Tompkins' book, cafe, who had offered her shelter. The first day Sami and Amber met, she was working the counter, and he fell in love with her the moment he laid eyes on her. That was three years earlier, and within a year of them meeting, they married and rented the upstairs apartment in a yellow house next to the liquor store. Amber's anxiety was slowly getting better with Sami, but there were still moments that taxed their relationship. Her anxieties would creep back in and she would close herself off from everyone, even Sami. There were times when she found it difficult to do much of anything. She would become emotional and lose her temper. Sami handled it the best he could, but near the end they almost broke up. When she died, he realized the drastic mistake he had almost made. He wondered what good was this new awareness when he had lost her anyway. It made him sick to think about it, but he hoped going back to work would help. And, yet, how does anyone recover from this deep a loss? He loved her so much. He had a deep need to do something, anything to take his mind off of things.

It seemed strange seeing the ferry terminal after the weeks away. The long ramp walkway on the plaza from Richmond Terrace to inside seemed to be further than he had remembered, and he felt a little jealous as a few skateboards whizzed past him, and then a girl flashed by on a power glider. He thought he just might have to get one of those once they stopped bursting into flames. The geek in him was seriously considering it.

In the terminal there were two giant fish tanks for people's amusement. As Sami stared at the fish, empathy kicked in, and he started to feel their sense of confinement. Such large fish in a large tank, but not nearly large enough for their size, it seemed cruel. There were announcements, but he didn't pay attention any longer, and they had all become a blur. If prompted however, it was likely he could recite them by heart. The two large doors opened and the crowd shuffled in and down the ramps to the boat with a sense of urgency. He resisted the impulse to let out a moo sound, but elected to silently feel like one of the cattle entering the barn. Staying away from the front and the crowds today, he was sure to lose his favorite seat. Sami always found comfort in routine. This attribute of his was one of the things that made him love Amber so much; it made him thirst for the contrast of her free spirit.

The ferry docked right on time and he shuffled off with the others. It was a mindless walk down to the 1 train, a transfer to the express at Chambers, and on to Times Square. When he stepped out on to the corner of 42$^{nd}$ street and 7$^{th}$ avenue he looked around and up in awe as he did so many times before.

Sami reached his office building on 6$^{th}$ avenue and 47$^{th}$ and walked past the usual guards with an invisible weight stretching high up to the top of the grand building entrance on his shoulders. He muttered good morning and pressed his badge to the sensor for the gate to open to the elevator banks and walked all the way to the last bank to his right. He was hoping to avoid seeing anyone who did know about Amber for at least a short while, but as he turned the corner into the already open car, there were two co-workers from accounting.

Rosa looked sadly at him. "Sami, we are so sorry to hear about your wife."

"Thanks, I appreciate your concern, and thank you for the flowers you sent to the service. Please tell Dennis too."

"We will. It's good to have you back. If you need anything, stop up."

The rest of the elevator ride up was in an awkward silence, with a few heavy breaths as if to say something, but then nothing. Sami nodded goodbye to his co-workers as he got off at the 36$^{th}$ floor and after grabbing coffee in the pantry, he went to his cubicle in a back area of the graphics workstations. No one else from his department had yet arrived. It was a relief. It would be the first time they would be seeing him since Amber's service and he knew it would be awkward. There were photos of Amber on his board in direct view so he moved them to the side board. He just wanted this day over.

On Staten Island, at the corner of Bay Street and Victory Boulevard, stood a long building that ran almost the length of the largest section of Tompkinsville Park. It was a two-story structure with a façade of mirrored glass. The glass panes so complete and the mirrors so clear that the entire building was like a reflection of the park. The bottom floor houses social services while the entire top floor had been gutted, and awaiting the start of a construction build-out.

Dr. Noah Braxton, a physicist and independent associate of IC&P, and his long-time friend, Adler Beaumont, a member of their business division, both in their early-thirties, were alone on the top level. Beaumont secured funding for a theoretical project for his friend even though Innovation Capital & Promotion (IC&P) was most concerned with profits. After all, it was mostly Noah's other projects that helped Adler climb the corporate ladder, making him sure to soon make VP. It was the least he could do. Noah already had his main equipment and most of what was needed; Adler merely had to call in favors. IC&P would pick up the tab for the power used from the local grid, and the cost of the car services and small research stipend for Noah.

Noah was tracing the steps through the expanse marking the spots where he was to place the projection towers for his experiment. It will be set up as a large footprint, rectangular in shape, so it would soon take up most of the cavernous floor. There will be four of the towers connected to the distribution feeds that were controlled by the systems rack. Power is to come from both the main source as well as the capacitors stored in large shipping containers already stacked out in the back parking lot since the week before. For a few weeks, it made the social services workers a little angry that they'd lost eight of their best parking spaces to make room for those containers.

"It took a lot of string pulling this time my friend. Do you realize how hard it was to get the tie-in from that carrier?"

"I do, Adler, and I appreciate it. This one may not be for profit, but you know I'll give you others."

"I have no doubt. Besides, we've been friends for a long time and you've done me more than enough favors. The carrier is docking tomorrow and they run the lines on Wednesday. They plan to finish the connections by Thursday morning. As you requested, the large scale capacitors stacked in the back lot were temporarily connected to the building grid so they can get a head start charging. They have been charging since they arrived. That is an acceptable load until the ship is tied in, and your control systems rack will remain on the building source. Those capacitors are on loan from SciLab, so make sure you thank Dr. Greene."

"I will. The movers are loading the rest of my gear in the freight and I should be set up in a day. Thanks for getting this space. This will do nicely."

"Sorry for the time constraints on the ship, but it was the best I could get. This place doesn't start construction for at least another six weeks, so I had no trouble securing it for your work."

"The time restrictions will do fine. I understand I cannot begin my full tests until after the services close downstairs, but I've run the numbers and with the time I'm given access to the ship's power generator, the pre-staging of the first charge, and the period needed for an additional charge, it will allow me to squeeze in a second chance to fire up my systems and perform additional tests while the ship is still docked. The capacitors must charge slowly so twice is all I will get though. Twice will be enough. I cannot thank you enough, Adler. Without that ship's generators, it wouldn't happen. The neighborhood could never hold the load during the test runs themselves."

"No neighborhood could. You're pulling a lot of juice. No worries. I'll check on you tomorrow or better yet, Wednesday when they begin running the cable. I'll get a chance to talk with Captain Lambertson. I've not seen him since we sponsored one of his public outreach projects.

Good PR never hurts, even for our beloved Navy. Let me know if you need anything else."

"Thanks, Adler."

"You know, I worked this out sight unseen, but what is it that you are really hoping to accomplish here with all this power? What is it that you think you will see?"

"On a tiny scale I was able to sustain a field that created a small number of ghost particles. With the right amount of resonate feedback and power, particles appeared from nowhere, and that's simply not possible. When the field was removed, they were gone, but I was certain for that time in that field they were there. It was just too tiny a sample size, but with the way the resonance field works, it couldn't be just slightly larger. I extrapolated the size area I would need and the power it would take to produce enough of a result to be more definitive. That's why I needed this large space, and that's why the ship's generator and SciLab's capacitors are keys to its success."

"I'm kind of sorry I asked. I still don't understand, but you have fun," Beaumont said, smiling.

"Sorry. I'll know more after this, and it may hold little to no practical application. Then again, it could lead to endless possibilities. And who knows, maybe one day a profit."

"Now *that* I understand. You keep coming up with those ideas, and I'll keep helping you make them happen. I will see you Wednesday before lunch. If you have time, we'll go for a bite to eat."

Sami's four co-workers had been to Amber's service, and now they welcomed him back one–by–one after his weeks out. First David, Nick and Aaron stopped by his desk. Sami thanked them. David told him to make it an easy day, and said they would cover as he brought himself up to speed. David ran the department and was Sami's direct supervisor, and Sami, Nick, Aaron and Leah were all graphic artists. Leah sat in the cubicle just beyond Sami's. After the others stepped away, she rolled her chair over next to Sami's and sat down. Leah was someone Sami had always confided in when he was having problems with Amber. She reached out and took his hand.

"I wanted to call you these weeks, Sami, but the guys told me you likely just wanted to be alone for a while. I'm sure they were right. How are you doing?"

"I'm doing okay. Ready to get back to work."

"Yeah. But how are you really doing?

Leah looked at him sternly. Sami dodged the question.

"I knew you were thinking about me, and thanks for picking up my work while I was gone. I left Nick hanging with the Elysium acquisition presentation. I bet he had so much trouble finding the files I already created that he had to start from scratch."

"He was fine. We all helped. We love you, Sami, and we care how you are doing."

Sami felt the sincerity in Leah. Leah was making it too easy to unload some of the anguish he was feeling, so he gave in.

"You know, Leah, we argued the morning she was killed. I can't believe I wasted our last days together. It took losing her to realize how much I loved her."

"I know you, and I felt it. I'm sure she knew it too. If there were two people better suited for each other than you two, I've never met them."

I understood what I was in for when I married her... I just stopped seeing her beauty and innocence. I should have just been there for her when she needed me. Amber was killed by a woman who had a heart attack behind the wheel. The woman died too. There is no one left alive to be angry with. I only blame myself for the way that I her before she died."

"I'm so sorry, Sami, but you don't have to blame yourself. I know she would never want you to feel this way. She may have had her moments. We all do. Whenever I saw her, Amber was always so nice."

"She was a reciprocator. Whatever she felt from you, she would always return. I miss her so much."

Leah gave Sami a long hug. When she finally rolled her chair back to her section, she gave him a look that needed no words.

His supportive co-workers picked up the slack while he spent most of the day reading through backed up emails and memos. Sami adjusted the best he could, and, by Tuesday late morning, he felt ready to pick up his first new assignment.

On Wednesday, his brother Sean would be meeting up with him so they could talk about him possibly moving up the hill. There were far too many memories in that apartment, and the lease was just about due. In the meantime, there were often apartments opening up in the building where Sean lived. Sean felt it would be nice to have his little brother so close, and Sami would be even closer to the ferry. It was on St Marks Place, a tree lined street just up the hill, and just around the corner from the St George Theater, a nice group of stores, restaurants and a popular pub, Steiny's. The public library he enjoyed was right around the corner as well.

Noah looked out the back window, where he could see the Navy personnel had begun to run the large black cables from the ship to the capacitor storage containers. Adler was down in the lot, talking with a man in uniform who was likely Captain Lambertson. He tried to make out the conversation and with the mirrored glass, he could see them clearly, but they could not see him. Adler, had always been personable and good at getting things done. Ever since their senior year of high school, Noah would come up with the ideas and Adler would negotiate the means to make them happen. They became fast friends when Noah helped Adler ace his grade on a team assignment in science class. Their friendship remained strong even throughout 4 years in different colleges. Their collaborations carried over into their professional careers. It was advantageous that Adler would land a job with a company that would make their fortune funding research and development to production. Meanwhile, Noah had such innovative and, mostly profitable ideas. It was his studies in quantum and theoretical physics that fueled his ideas for innovations in technologies. Adler helped him guide those innovations into practical applications for profit.

The projection towers were precisely three meters tall, set up in the four corners. All of the flight cases were opened and assembled into an amble control station to the side. All that was left to do was to mount and position all the testing and monitoring probes and cameras. Once completed, Noah could begin the tedious task of all the micro calibrations needed to fix the tower positions precisely. Since the control station ran on building power, he could begin calibrating his equipment while waiting for the ship's connection to the charge bank and parallel main. None of that would take more than a day, so it would be moments of anxiety until his first test on Friday.

Noah heard the echo of the freight elevator door close downstairs and the sound of the lift coming up. The door opened, and, in walked Adler and the man from the lot. From the distance, the man looked a bit confused, but intrigued.

When they got closer, Adler introduced, "Noah, this is Captain Joseph Lambertson from the U.S. Navy. He was the one who got the approval for you to tie into the ship's generator for the next two weeks. Like me, I'm sure he won't understand what this thing is, but he'd really like to have a look regardless."

"Thank you so much, Captain," Noah said, reaching out his hand

"Please, call me Joe. So, Adler tells me you are looking for ghosts," Captain Lambertson grinned.

Noah laughed, "Well, not exactly, but I guess you can say that."

"Well, it's not exactly Navy business, but when Adler told me you were responsible for the enhancements to our new control room night vision monitors, I was happy to help. They are a vast improvement over the old ones, and the resolution is tremendous. They were a major advantage for us in the last war games maneuvers. During simulation, we beat every other ship when we attacked at night. With the old equipment, that might not have been an option. You're a brilliant scientist, Adler tells me. After using your monitor designs, I would agree. I hope you can get what you need in the time we have at dock."

"I hope so too. Thank you."

"You do understand the full power needed during the test runs can only be maintained for 30 minutes at a time before we throttle down the generators? Your tests require us to run at the top limit of the generator's design specifications, and I'm anxious to test it at full capacity. But there are limits."

"I understand. That will work fine."

"Maybe you can explain your project a little for Joe?" Adler asked.

Noah powered up the control station and tried his best to interpret what they saw on the various monitors and what it was he was hoping to accomplish. He was animated, walking them to the closest tower and explaining the mechanism inside and the purpose for the various components. Within minutes, Noah watched Beaumont's and Lambertson's eyes glazed over. He sat down in the main chair, spun around and asked if there were any questions. There were none. When the Captain hinted that he needed to return to the ship, Noah could not thank him enough as he walked him to the freight.

Calibrations would not be excessively difficult to complete. With little left to do, Noah accepted Adler's suggestion to go for a cup of coffee. Across the park was a small bookstore coffee shop, so they decided they would go there. The smell of coffee and pastries was in the air from the moment they stepped in. It was a long space, with non-matching tables in the front section and a small, rounded stage opposite the serving counter. The menus hanging high on the back wall behind the counter were a mix of printed items and hand written menus for the daily specials. The floor was plywood, stained red, with a pattern in the natural wood tones that looked like a red river flowing. There were high side-counters and bar stools with computers for Internet access. In the back, was a small set of stairs that lead up to the bathroom to the right and all the bookshelves in the back. It had an almost 1960's atmosphere, with album covers and posters filling the walls next to paintings hung, and for sale by local artists. Most notably, everyone inside, including the owners, seemed to dress to match the era. To the left, facing the counter, up high was a sign, reading 'There are no strangers here... Only friends we have not met'. Noah felt it was a comfortable friendly atmosphere, while Adler, being more highbrow, thought he'd stepped onto the island of misfit toys.

Of the dozen or so small tables for two or four people, about half were filled with mostly young people drinking coffee as they read or used the free Wi-Fi with their smartphones and laptops. There was a cute young girl of perhaps nineteen years old behind the counter and the bohemian looking couple, in their 40's was tending to the books. They ordered two coffees and two slices of raspberry apple pie, and Noah brought the tray to the table while Adler stayed behind to pay. The young lady behind the counter was a bit flustered by Adler's glare, and the older woman noticed so she came over to assist. She was protective of her, almost motherly. Adler even realized he was being a little creepy, so he made sure to leave a five in the tip jar. For some strange reason, he believed money made up for anything.

"Still scaring the young waitresses, Adler?"

He chuckled, "You know how it is."

"No, not really. But, I know you, old friend."

"So, you agreed to coffee. I guess things are coming along."

"They are. Since the capacitors are already charging, I'll be ready for the first run after closing this Friday. The office and counter workers downstairs finish at 3 on Fridays. The cleaning crew leaves by 5, so I planned my test run to start at 6. Given the capacitors need to charge very slowly, it will take most of a week to ready them again. Even still, that gives me one more run, and I will schedule that the following Friday for the same time. If successful, I will have a wealth of data to mine. Since I could never keep up with what will be coming in, I'll be recording every measurement I can."

Noah noticed the man who looked to own the shop sitting at the next table, peering overly curiously. Looking the part of the scientist and the businessman that they both were, they did stand out. Neither of their types ever frequented the place, but they also seemed like an odd match for friends.

"New to the neighborhood?" the man asked.

He turned his chair slightly to face the two. Noah noticed there were books on Mysticism and Spirituality on the table in front of the man, and then spied a shelf full of books on these subjects nearby.

"I will be working on a project in that building on the corner across the street for a couple of weeks. My name is Noah. This is my friend, Adler."

"I'm Stewart. My wife, Halie, over there, and I, own this shop."

"Well, the pie is amazing, and the coffee is really good," said Adler.

Noah agreed.

"So, what kind of project is it? What do you two do?"

"Well, Adler here is in business, and won't be staying. He's just visiting. The project I'm working on is based on theoretical physics. It's a bit complicated."

"Oh, you're a scientist," Stewart said with a little smirk.

Noah didn't want to be dismissive, but it was not an easy subject to discuss, as witnessed during his attempts to explain it to Adler and the captain.

"Well, I'll be back for pie. Maybe when we have more time, I can try to explain it to you."

"Whatever it is, I'm sure something else will come along to make it wrong. You know science. One day something is true and the next it's all wrong. I never put my faith in science."

"Well that's not exactly how it works. Most times we build on existing knowledge, but, yes, you are right that science is meant to be self-correcting. That's a good thing."

Stewart held up his books on Metaphysics.

"I read these books for knowledge. Scientists think they have all the answers."

"That's not true - we don't have all the answers, but we do have the best ones."

Stewart looked as if he would respond, but instead he turned his chair back and continued reading. Noah and Adler returned to their conversation.

"So, that's quite a bit of power there. You're sure you won't turn the neighborhood into a rather large crater, right?" Adler asked.

"I'm sure," Noah said laughing. "Maybe just fry myself."

"You're joking, right?"

It was 6:00 on Wednesday, and Sean was on the park bench on the corner of Bay Street and Victory Boulevard, waiting for Sami to walk down from the ferry after work. He was helping his little brother find a suitable place to move to when his lease went up in just a matter of weeks. A few minutes later, he saw Sami walking closer just beyond the Key Foods store. He could tell his brother was still feeling emotional by the look Sami could not help but have, and the way he looked only down. Sami finally looked up as he crossed, and saw Sean waiting.

"So, how are you feeling, little brother?"

"Besides the fact that you chose to wait for me right where Amber always did, I guess okay," Sami said and smiled.

"Oh, sorry, Sami, I really am."

"No worries, big brother. I'm okay. I've resigned myself to the fact that she'd never be waiting here for me again."

"Well, I should have just waited in the coffee shop."

"It wouldn't help. You know that's where we met. Everything here reminds me of her."

"That's why we need to get you an apartment up the hill and away from this park. It's not that the hurt will ever go away, but putting a little distance between you and the memories might help. Of course not right away, but once you're settled, there are a couple of women at the office, Julie and Casey, and we can double date. It would be good for you to socialize again. What do you say?"

"I can't think about that right now. Let's get that apartment though. What did the super tell you? Is there anything available?"

"He believes apartment 208 is freeing up, but he can't tell me until Saturday. If it is, you'll need to grab it right away. The Bayview House is a nice building and the apartments go fast."

"Thanks, I have some money put aside so I can put a deposit on it and submit my application as soon as you find out. Thanks, Sean."

"What are brothers for?"

"So you really like it there?"

"The super is great, pleasant tenants, a laundry room in the basement and I know you don't need it, but there is a garage for my car. I don't know why you gave up yours."

"It was just an added expense. You know Amber couldn't drive with her anxiety and I walk to the ferry. We just didn't need one."

"And you work in Manhattan."

"I've always considered St George to be an extension of lower Manhattan, and now with the wheel and mall coming there will finally be a real connection to New York City. I like the area fine. I just need to get a little further from these memories."

"Well, you will find that the top of the hill is quite a different place than down here, and you'll be next to the green market that sets up in the St George Theater parking lot on Saturdays. I'm really glad you are taking my suggestion. It will be good for you. Come over on Saturday, and let's talk with the super. This way if the apartment does become available, we can get the application for the management company right away. On Sunday, maybe we can go to those museums you like in Snug Harbor."

"I would like that. Thanks Sean."

"So, how were your first few days back?"

"The first day was the toughest, but yesterday was better and today even better than Tuesday. I'm getting to whatever my new normal will be."

"And when you are not at work, how are you feeling?"

"For a few weeks up until she died, I treated her so badly, and it makes me sick to my stomach. I just can't shake the thought of how we fought before she went out for her walk the day she was killed. I must have made her feel so bad that day."

"You couldn't have known. You can't beat yourself up over it."

"No, but now I understand just how much I loved her and how dumb I was to be willing to give her up. I'll never get the chance to resolve that, to tell her how much she meant to me."

"I'd say something spiritual, but you and I both know that's never been a strong subject for me."

"You're right. Please don't," Sami said, finally smiling.

"Come on, I'll buy you a coffee."

They walked through the park to the coffee shop and stood outside for a moment. It was his first time there since Amber had been killed. Halie, the shop owner, knew Sami and Amber had been arguing before Amber's accident. Having always mothered her, she had been angry with Sami. She was fine at the service, but he wondered about how she'd be now. He was a little apprehensive about going in, but when he finally did, Halie came right up and hugged him, wiping away tears. Stewart also came over to greet Sami. Halie's anger with him had turned into empathy.

She pointed to a girl behind the counter and said, "This is Melissa. She started this week. Melissa, this is Sami and Sean Bell. Brothers, as you can tell."

"Nice to meet you both. My friends call me Lis."

Sean reached out, "Nice to meet you, Lis."

Sami felt a little uncomfortable looking at her since she was standing in the spot where Amber was when they first met. When Lis did make eye contact, she fixed her eyes in a dare for him to keep looking. She thought he was cute and wasn't going to let him get away without looking into her eyes.

While still looking at Sami, she asked, "So what can I get for you?"

18

"Just two small cups of coffee, please."

Lis rang them up, smiling as she handed them the cups. Halie and Stewart walked Sean and Sami to a table near the back, and, after one more hug, they left them alone.

"She's really cute, huh?"

"Sean, you're twenty-five. Lis looks to be about nineteen, maybe twenty at most."

"That's not such a big gap. Besides, she is obviously interested in you."

"Just stop," Sami said, grinning.

"Well, at least I got you in a better mood.

"That you did, big brother."

It was one more hurdle to overcome, being in the café, but Sami soon felt comfortable enough in there. He and Sean sat and talked for over a half hour and had a coffee refill before they said their goodbyes to Halie and Stewart and started to walk out. When Sami passed the counter, he turned to say goodbye to Lis. She reached out and took his arm.

"You'll come back, I hope?"

"Yes, of course. I live next door. I'll be back."

"Take care, Lis," Sean added.

They stepped out the door and Sean walked left to go up the hill, while Sami turned right toward his apartment. Both turned back to look at each other for a moment.

"I saw that. I told you she likes you. Stay happy, Sami."

"Thanks for being there for me, big brother."

It was early Thursday morning when Noah got the call from Joe Lambertson that the power was connected and ready to go. He verified his meters and switched on the feed to the banks of capacitors. Since it would take them close to a week to trickle charge they had been charging from the main power grid until the ship was brought online. It was a smaller amount of power, but coming from the neighborhood grid meant IC&P was paying the bill. It was still necessary since it meant he would be ready for the first run the next evening. He forwarded the schedule to the ship's commander. They would need to keep a small steady flow of power to charge the capacitors for the second run, but Noah would need all the power the ship generators could provide once he switched on the field for the next two Fridays from 6:00 PM until 6:30. It was agreed that they would run the generators at maximum capacity during those windows.

He went over every control system and checked every video camera, microphone and matter sensor surrounding his inner field space. Then he turned the one camera in the control area to himself and clicked to record.

"Thursday, May 19th 2016. I am Dr. Noah Braxton. Tomorrow evening at 6:00 PM, I will be performing the first of two controlled experiments searching for signs of phantom matter. In a smaller experiment four years ago at the Cal-Tech labs, I accidentally stumbled on what looked to be new matter present in the center of the focal area. Based on the resonance numbers in the first experiment, in order to get real results, I needed an exponential jump in power and size of the subject area. I have assembled the four transmitter towers in the room and they all tie into this master control system. The distances and power output will be listed in the included record. First, it takes a burst of power stored in the capacitor banks in order to start the resonance regeneration, and then the main power goes online. That sustains the field. I have not yet formulated a hypothesis for where these ghost particles come from, or where they return when the field is turned off. My hope is to compile enough data during the two thirty-minute periods in the weeks ahead to keep scientists busy for some time, although I plan to take a look at the data first before showing it to anyone else. Step one is to determine if what the equipment showed originally is actually there. Step two is to make sense of what I find."

Many possibilities went through his mind. He knew that dark matter revealed itself through gravitational influence, yet no one knew what it really was, or where it was. He knew that dark energy revealed itself because of its influence on the acceleration of the expansion of the universe, yet no one knows what that really was either. Whatever he discovered at Cal-Tech, it was certainly profound. Maybe he found a way to make dark matter visible, or maybe it was something else that was as of yet unexplainable.

Noah carefully documented and adjusted every setting and performed every calibration. Using a precise laser measuring tool, he fine-tuned and recorded all the distances between the towers then locked them into place. Once he ported all the distances and calibration numbers into the database, there was not much more that could be done until his first test window the next evening.

Lis finished carrying a tray with two lattes, and two mega hummus bagels to the furthest table, and, seeing no one waiting for service, she sat down at the table where Halie was. Lis looked at Halie as if she had something to say, but stayed silent for a moment.

"Halie, what do you think of the brothers that came in yesterday? I could tell you cared about the one you hugged."

"I like them both very much. Stewart and I have been concerned about Sami, the one I hugged. He lost his wife to an accident just a few weeks ago and that was the first time he's been back in here since she died."

"Oh my God. I kind of flirted with him a little."

"It's okay. I'm sure he took it as a compliment. You must have seen how he looked a little lost."

"That made him even more attractive," Lis said with a tiny smile.

"Well, now they are both unattached. Sean has never been married. I think he's twenty-five. Sami just turned twenty-four. We had his birthday party here just two weeks before Amber was killed. There's something else I should tell you."

"What?" Lis asked softly.

"He met his wife here, working like you behind the counter, so don't take it personally if he finds it hard looking directly at you. We weren't sure he could bear the memory coming in at all, so it was nice to see him come in. His brother Sean is doing his best to look out for him, and Sami is lucky to have him. Poor Amber. She was so beautiful - like a daughter to me. When she came into our lives, she was so troubled, so full of emotional scars and riddled with anxiety. Sami was the greatest thing that ever happened to her, and he loved her so much. He changed her life in the best way. Not everything was perfect though. During the two years married, she had lingering anxiety issues, but she was improving with the help of therapy. Sami always had the patience of a saint."

"I noticed he was a bit shy."

"Not normally. He'll warm up. He's just not yet himself, but I'm glad you are interested in Sami. He could use all the friends he can get right now."

"I understand. I hope you don't think badly of me, but I kind of like Sami, and I can be patient. Maybe one day he could fall for another counter girl," Lis said.

"I told you that I care for Sami very much and he deserves to be happy again one day. That saying is total bunk. Time heals nothing completely, but, at least, scars grow over the wounds. You may be waiting for some time though. Sean told me last week that Sami was taking it all really hard. He's young and resilient, but it may be awhile before he even looks at anyone else."

The ferry docked and Sami had conquered his fourth day back to work, and endured the commute home. He felt as though he was getting back to normal, but walking down Bay Street, he was reminded of personal issues yet to be resolved, and living in their apartment would be putting a damper on that for the near future. This time, when he reached the park he saw the bench was empty. When he reached it, he sat down, careful to leave the spot where Amber always sat. He thought of how he would be moving soon. He thought about how much he still missed her, how much he still loved her. Within moments, he felt overcome with grief, and he spoke out softly, begging to be heard.

*"I wish you hadn't left me, Amber. I miss you so much and I can't imagine life without you. I am so sorry we argued the last time we were together. It was wrong to pressure you, and you were doing so well. I don't know what came over me... the pressures of work, maybe just*

*some built up stress. I only wish I had gotten the chance to make it up to you. I never meant to hurt you and I hope you know, or I hope you can hear me now. You know I never believed in the supernatural, but at your service Stewart said you are still with us, and that you are going to help me get through this. But God damn it, Amber. I don't want to get through this. I didn't want to lose you in the first place. I want to wake up and have it be just a nightmare."*

Sami wiped tears away on his sleeve, and quickly took his sunglasses out of his bag, putting them on to hide his swollen eyes. He noticed an old woman on a bench nearby who was crying too. She was staring down at her feet with a look of disbelief and she continued to quietly sob. He felt horrible for her, but felt helpless in his own sorrow. He would have been the first to try and comfort her if he hadn't been in such a sad state himself. Instead, he walked past her slowly wondering where her anguish was coming from.

Passing the coffee shop, he stopped for a moment, but didn't go in. He could see Halie and Lis sitting in the back and they noticed him by the window. Halie made a gesture, asking if he was coming in, but Sami just waved hello and continued on to his apartment. He did manage a small smile before turning away.

He unlocked the door and threw his laptop bag on the chair next to the desk in the entrance area. It was so quiet in the apartment, so he turned on the television hoping it might distract him from his thoughts. Then he noticed there was a stack of boxes against the wall that his landlord, Julia, promised to bring up from the basement. She was a nice woman, and she offered them so he could finally start packing Amber's possessions away. It would be the hardest task that he could think of. It made him cry when he removed her makeup and other items from the dresser, so he only imagined how hard it would be to pack her clothes childhood photo albums, and the photos of them together.

He would keep some of the most recent things, but he planned to give the ones from her childhood to Amber's sister, Ruth. He assembled the first flattened box and took it into the bedroom to at least start, but within minutes his heart was breaking even more. Packing all of her things away was so final. He knew he could not ask Ruth. She was as overwhelmed by the loss of Amber as he was. Then he thought he might ask Halie if she knew anyone he might hire to do it for him.

Sami walked down the steps and back next door to the coffee shop. When he walked in, Lis smiled and said hello. Halie came over and hugged him. She realized immediately that it may not be the right thing to continue given it was a reminder of the reason for her concern.

"Halie, I have to pack Amber's things away and it's just a little more than I can bear at the moment. Would you know of someone I could hire to do it for me? Some of the items need to be sorted, but it should not take more than a visit or two."

Lis was listening and Sami had his back to her talking to Halie, so she gestured to Halie that she would like to do it for him.

"Sure, I do. What about Melissa? She could use some extra money."

"Are you sure it would be okay to ask?"

"You would be doing her a favor if you asked her. She's been wanting more hours here that we can't give her."

Halie grabbed Sami by the hand and walked him over to Lis at the counter who had turned away to make believe she wasn't listening.

"Melissa, Sami needs some chores done and I was thinking that you could use some extra money. What do you think?"

Lis smiled, but stifled it knowing the reason why Sami was asking.

"Yes, I would like to help. Just let me know what needs to be done," she said looking at Sami.

"Thanks, that's great. I have to be there in case you have questions, but when are you free? I am busy with my brother this weekend, but can you come on a weekday after work?"

"I am off from here tomorrow, so I won't be in the neighborhood, and I have an appointment after work on Monday. I could start on Tuesday. Would that be okay for you?"

"Tuesday works fine. You might need a little more time on Wednesday if you are free to finish then."

"Wednesday is fine too."

"Thank you, Lis. The job is to pack some clothes and personal items that belonged to my wife, and I need them to be carefully sorted. She was killed a few weeks ago and it is too emotional for me at the moment. Would that be okay?"

"I am so sorry for your loss, Sami. I will take the best care in packing her things. If you need other things done, please ask. If you need help cleaning, or doing laundry, you can hire me for those as well."

"Thanks again. You reminded me that my place hasn't been cleaned in weeks, so please excuse the mess there. You can understand why I've not been motivated to do much of anything as of late. We can talk about that when you come over on Tuesday."

"You live nearby, right?"

"I live right next door to the liquor store in the upstairs apartment of the yellow house. Don't worry. I'll walk over and get you. What time do you get off?"

"Well, this time, actually, 7:00."

"Then 7:00 it is. See you Tuesday."

Sami thanked Halie and returned to his apartment, knowing he would not have to endure the barrage of memories that would come from packing Amber's things. He would just need to overlook them for now, thankful that she had her own closet. Feeling a little guilty for his lack of cleaning, he took time to spot clean his kitchen and bathroom. At least he would not be overly embarrassed when Lis came to help. His bed, however, always remained unmade. Amber was the one who would make it every morning. Some of his best habits were really hers, and now it was obvious. After straightening up those two rooms, Sami finally went to relax. Since Amber died, he only wanted to come home and sleep. It meant less time to think and he could at least still see her in his dreams.

Noah arrived at the site at noon on Friday, which was a bit later than the other days because he would be staying late. Monday, when they first came, he had been driven by Beaumont, but since then he was taking the Staten Island Ferry across. Since he lived in Cobble Hill, in Brooklyn, it was an easy hop on the R train to Whitehall Street at the South Ferry Station, but when he left in the evening he would use the car service IC&P provided to take him home.

His footsteps echoed in the cavernous space as he walked over to the first flight case. In that case was a small refrigerator filled with a few snacks and bottled water. Next to it were some additional items such as glasses, utensils and towels to make the work space more livable. He purchased a bottle of red from Honor Wines just outside the ferry terminal on Bay Street, so he pulled it from the bag and placed it in the refrigerator to chill. Once the test window launched and the equipment started to monitor and record, there would be nothing to do but watch and wait for the run to end. The whole process was automated, so a glass of Pinot Noir just might come in handy later. For now, though, he pulled out and opened a bottle of water to drink. It was right at the moment that he sat at his station that a video request came on the screen from Beaumont.

"Hey, Adler, I just arrived a second ago."

"Don't worry, I won't keep you long. I just want to wish you luck. I know how important this is to you."

"It is, and I owe you another one now," Noah said smiling.

"I know that look. We've already lost track of who owes who long ago. I know you will have a lot of residual work to do on this when your tests are complete, but you have to pay your bills. When you're ready, I have a proposal for you. It's a really quick consultation role right up your alley and for SciLab too, and you owe them. So, are you all set there?"

"I was just about to check. Stay on for a moment... It looks like the capacitors are just about charged. Joe gave me a test boost yesterday on the mains and that went well. It's nice to have so much power on hand."

"Well, don't get used to it. You don't get to tap into a docked carrier's power generation plant just any time you want my friend," Adler said with a slight laugh.

"Well, if this ends up producing something extraordinary, and especially if there is a possibility of profit, they may just build me my own power plant," Noah laughed back.

"That they would. If it makes money, they are in all the way. It's why I like working at IC&P. They never mind taking chances, and in the end, they always come out ahead. One thing is for sure: they are impressed with you already. Keep it up and you'll write your own ticket."

"Listen, you are welcome to join me later this evening for the test. I plan to uncork a bottle of wine after to celebrate."

"I can't tonight. The wife has a party she's dragging me to. I'll come out next Friday and have a look. So you sure you're not going to crater the neighborhood right?" Alder said with a jokingly serious face.

"I'll try not to. So that's why you're coming next week instead. You want to see if I blow the place up first."

"Are you kidding me? I'd rather blow myself up with you than attend this party Nancy has us going to. Speaking of the wife, she has another friend she thinks you'd like. I'm really sorry, but she's got it bad when it comes to wanting to marry you off. This one is kind of cute. I think you'd like her."

"I liked the last friend, Donna, she tried to match me with, but we just didn't quite click. Love and dating are funny things. There's no real formula, and it's something even we scientists can't seem to explain," Noah said smiling.

"You'll get there, but only if you socialize once in a while. You spend too much damn time in your labs. So humor Nancy, okay?"

"Sure, anything to keep peace in your marriage, my friend."

"Don't think I don't appreciate that. Okay, I'll let you get to work. This is your day. Good luck, Noah."

Sami packed up his laptop and wished his co-workers a nice weekend before getting in the elevator to leave. He had made it through his first week back and was glad that at least his work was a respite. The others there had consoled him enough and he was almost back up to speed with the projects. It was just what he needed to help him move on. He walked down 7th avenue past the dozens of Elmos, Batmen and other characters, but realized he was staring at the painted women just a little too long. Two came over and wrapped their arms around him, each looking for five dollars. He thanked them for the attention and checked to see if any red, white or blue rubbed off on him, then continued down to the 42nd street subway station.

While his time away initially forced him from his normal routine, by this trip he had returned to his organized behavior. He walked the platform to the far end and stood at the red call box, knowing that when he caught the 2 or 3 express, that door would let him out right at the correct door to the 1 train. That was the rear door of car 3 and it let him off right by the stairs leading up to the ferry. Once again, without thinking, he reverted to habit. As usual he was early for the 5:30 ferry. He would reach Staten Island by 5:50 or 5:55.

The weekend would be tough, but at least he would spend it with Sean and that would keep his mind off Amber a little bit. He felt so conflicted because, on one hand, he wanted to cherish all the memories. On the other hand, it was painful. He sat for almost 15 minutes, checking his iPhone, and then got up to stand near the door to beat the crowd. There was nothing worse than getting stuck in back of the pack as you exit the boat. He acknowledged a few of the usual people already standing in front and waited patiently to dock. There were the announcements again, which he ignored, and he could smell the salt water that kicked up in front as the engines slowed to dock.

As they shuffled off, the tourists circled back into the terminal, most of the others headed up bus ramps and down to the train, but Sami and a few others walked the ramp to Richmond Terrace, and to Bay Street. His mind was in a fog as he advanced down Bay on auto-pilot.

Noah got the ping from the ships engineer that the power was going to flow as scheduled beginning at 6:00 PM. He meticulously programed every step into a well-designed macro. At the press of a single engage button, a carefully orchestrated sequence of rotations between towers begins, with the first step to lock in the order. At that point, the capacitor feed opens with a burst of power to the electromagnetic center rods in each tower. A regenerative resonance is created and the main feed from the ship's generators keeps it going until the load shuts down after the 30 minutes he is given. It was almost time and he could just about hear his heart beat. He turned on the initial controls to wait for the verification of the power to the feed to start.

At 6:00 PM, the meter lit showing the power was live on the wire. Noah pressed the engage button and in moments, it went from the initial rotation to the burst, then to the field generation. There was a strange audible choir of soft tones that filled the room, and echoed in the vast space. It sounded like thousands of soft whispers. The room glowed with a low blue hue and Noah saw particles of matter bouncing around inside the target area, which registered as new. His initial readings showed the same new particle generation as he had seen during his small scale experiment, but this time they filled the entire space within the towers, and they were visible to the naked eye as miniscule sparkling points. Each particle, with a hint of blue that suspended in the deep black in the center of the towers collectively gave it that hue. They seemed to appear from nowhere. Noah checked to make sure all the monitoring and testing equipment were running, and recording everything. He didn't want to miss a moment he'd be given.

Sami approached and noticed a strange soft blue haze all around the park as he stepped onto the sidewalk after crossing Victory Boulevard. Once inside and embedded in it, it became less noticeable, but it was a most curious thing. A woman's laugh caught his attention and he noticed it was the old woman that he saw crying just the day before. Today, she was laughing as a small dog repeatedly jumped on and off her lap. He was glad that whatever had caused the pain yesterday wasn't long-lived. Still focused on the woman, he passed the first benches in a daze, when he heard his name.

"Sami, where are you going? I'm right here."

Sami turned to see Amber sitting in the spot on that first bench where she had always waited. He thought it had to be a dream, so he closed his eyes and wiped them. When he reopened them, she was still there. Tears welled up and he sat down folding his arms around her and hugged her tightly. He kissed her cheeks repeatedly then pressed his head on her shoulder, ear to ear. She could hear him crying softly and then spoke still in his arms.

"So, I guess you're not still mad at me?" she asked in her gentlest voice.

"I missed you so much. I don't understand. I don't…"

Sami realized that if he tried to tell Amber the truth about what had happened, she would just be frightened. He stopped talking, stopped thinking, and hugged and kissed her. When he finally came up for air, he looked at her and smiled.

"You were really mad at me this morning. When you told me you needed to think about things, I thought you would come home and tell me you were leaving me," she said.

"I'm so sorry, Amber. In the last weeks, I've realized even more how much I love you. I love you more than I ever had the strength to say."

Sami sat and listened as Amber talked about the recent past as if she was never killed. He thought he might be losing his mind. She was right here in front of him. He kissed her. She was real. Amber described a progression in the troubles they were having before she was killed, but in his memories, they had never happened. She was describing a Sami that he had since felt disappointed in.

"Amber, remember that argument we had a few weeks ago that morning before you went for your long walk?"

"The first one?" she asked back.

"There were more…? Oh, never mind. I love you, Amber, and I can't imagine not being with you. You have been through so much in your life and I need you to know that I understand. I need to just be there for you when you feel vulnerable like you still sometimes do."

Tears welled up in Amber's eyes, and she started to cry.

"I love you too, Sami. I don't mean to hurt you or push you away. I just can't help getting anxious, but I'm trying my best."

"Amber, never leave me."

"I won't. You had *me* worried that you were leaving."

Sami wondered if when they got home, it would be as if she had never been killed, and no one but he would know. This time, he didn't care; he just held her tightly, and with her head on his chest, he kissed her head. From his angle he looked down to see her eyes closed and warm smile. He was happy to just hold her for as long as he could, and did not let her go. Somehow, he was being given another chance, and this time, things would be different. He would make sure to show her every day just how much he loved her.

Before he realized, it was almost 6:30, and Amber gestured they should leave. They looked in each other's eyes and smiled, then held hands to walk the paved path toward their apartment. When they reached the edge of the park, just across from the coffee shop Sami looked ahead for just a moment, and felt Ambers hand slip from his. He turned back. She was gone.

Dr. Noah Braxton had had an incredibly successful run, and he texted Adler to that effect. Adler, having been forced to attend a party he had no interest in, texted back, 'help me'. Noah smiled as he performed the routines to button up the systems and lock up for the night. He pulled out the bottle of wine and set it on the table. There was just one more task before he could celebrate. He flipped the switch to transfer the steady power from the generator feed to the capacitor bank that began the almost week long recharge, but when he did, the feed cover blew off twenty feet into the air and the arc caused a bolt of power to strike the metal rim on the table next to him. One more inch and he would have electrocuted himself just as he had joked to Adler. He had neglected to fully lock down the cover shield, so he took time to put on rubber gloves and bolt that into place. He powered up the console one last time to make sure it was undamaged, and it was.

Now he could celebrate. Although the composition was yet unclear, the results were definitive. There was something there. Now he needed to find out what it was and where it came from. He pulled the cork from the bottle and poured one glass while waiting for the car service home. When it arrived, he brought the bottle and glass down with him to the car.

Overwhelmed with a new wave of grief, Sami sat on the curb and tears fell from his eyes. He buried his head in his hands, his elbows into his thighs, and pressed his shoes hard into the street. Now angry, he stood up and walked across to the coffee shop, opened the door, and stood just inside. He saw Halie and Stewart behind the counter.

"Did you see Amber?" he asked.

Customers at the tables looked curiously. Stewart and Halie were speechless for a moment, now with sad shocked looks on their faces, but he continued.

"She was just in the park. I saw her and talked with her. I even held her, and I kissed her, and now she's gone."

Halie walked over to hug Sami.

"Amber is gone, Sami, remember?" Halie said, now embracing him.

"But I saw her just now. I did. She was waiting for me in the park, on the bench where she would always sit."

"I believe you," Stewart said.

"I wanted so badly to tell her how sorry I was, and how much I love her, and now I got to," Sami said, sitting down at the first empty table.

Halie sat in the other chair with him and Stewart came around the counter and stood close.

"Maybe it was a gift, a second chance. Maybe her spirit didn't want to leave until she heard that from you," Stewart said with authority.

"I got to tell her how sorry I was, but I can't believe I had her back, and now she's gone again. Please don't tell Sean about this! Please, don't tell anyone. I don't want Sean worrying any more than he is already. He'll think I've completely lost my mind… Have I?"

Stewart brought a coffee over for Sami and Halie sat with him until he calmed. Sami seemed so conflicted—sad one moment and a little happy the next. He was convinced it was real, but how? And where did she go?

The cell phone rang and, Sami, still in bed, reached over, accidentally knocking it to the floor. He reluctantly sat up and reached down to retrieve and answer it.

"Hey, are you coming over soon?" Sean asked.

"Wait, what time is it?"

"It's almost 10:30, and the super leaves for Manhattan at noon. I haven't seen him yet this morning, so I don't know yet if the apartment is available, but come over anyway. We can look at Gateway next door if not. If it is, he can give you the application."

Sami, still half asleep, told his brother he would get there soon, and went into the bathroom to shower. The more awake he felt, the more he wondered if last night seeing Amber could have been a dream. He was so sure he had held her, and wondered himself if he were losing his mind. Maybe this was how powerful grieving could get. Maybe he had just pulled her from the depths of his grieving soul, so he could get the chance to tell her how sorry he was.

He walked up from his apartment to Victory Boulevard, along the park, and from the distance, he stared at the bench where Amber would sit when she waited for him. It was a quick walk up St Marks Place to Sean's apartment, on a nice street mostly filled with old colonial homes of various types, some recently restored. There were more trees on St Marks than there were in the entire Tompkinsville Park. When he arrived, Sean buzzed him in. The elevator door opened on 4 and Sean was already in the hall, looking toward the elevator. He held his door open until Sami went in.

"I'm expecting Rohan, the super, to call back. Do you want some coffee? Can I make you a sandwich?"

"Sure, I'll have coffee, and whatever you're having. Sorry, I woke late. I had a rough night."

Sami followed Sean into the kitchen.

"I understand. So, if apartment 208 doesn't open up, like I said, we can go next door. It's a much larger building and there is always something available."

"Well, to tell you the truth, I'm having second thoughts about leaving the apartment."

"Wow, what brought that on?"

"I don't know, Sean. I still miss her, but I feel a little better about Amber. There is something about that apartment and that park. I have help packing her things, and once that's done, I want to see how I feel. It won't be too long before I can buy something anyway, so maybe I can stick it out."

"Well, that's sudden, but whatever you think is best."

Sami didn't want to tell Sean his second thoughts were because of his encounter with Amber. If there was a possibility he could talk with her again, he would not want to jeopardize that. Several times, Sami resisted an urge to tell his brother that he had spoken with Amber, but then played out every scenario of Sean's reaction in his mind and none of them went well. Sean got the call that 208 would not be free, but it mattered little now.

They spent the next hours relaxing in Sean's living room. At his brother's place he felt so at home that when Sean left the room for a moment, Sami opened the window and went out to sit on the fire escape to stare at the city. He could see the Staten Island ferry boats crossing both ways in the harbor, and he watched the huge storage container ships go by assisted by various colored tug boats. From up there, the boat horns would echo against the Gateway apartment building next door in quite a calming way. He saw the giant overhead lights being tested at the Staten Island Yankees stadium just before he was ready to go back inside.

"I love sitting out there too," Sean said as Sami crawled back inside.

"It's really calming."

"Can I make you something to eat for dinner?"

"No, thank you. I have to stop at Key Foods for some things. I think I will head out now. Thanks for everything."

"You know it, little brother."

Sean opened the door, and when Sami walked into the hall, he turned back for a moment.

"Sean, when we die, do you think part of us remains?"

"You mean like a spirit?"

"Well, no, yeah… maybe. Just something."

"I don't know. I don't think anyone really knows for sure what happens."

"I used to ignore anything without proof, you know the things that Stewart believes in. But I'm not so sure any more."

"Is there something you want to talk about?" Sean said, seeing Sami's look of puzzlement.

"No, I'm fine. I'm just thinking that somehow Amber knows now how much I love her. I'm starting to think, well, it would be nice if she could."

"I'm sure she knew, little brother. Don't forget. We're going to the Staten Island Museum tomorrow, and that other one you like, Noble. I'll pick you up just before noon."

Sami walk down the staircase next the elevator this time, out onto St Marks and down Hyatt Street toward Bay Street to stop for groceries.

Adler, curious about the details, came to the test site and badged the freight elevator to the 2$^{nd}$ floor. It was just after 9:00 on Monday morning, and Noah was already at his workstation, examining the data with a smile on his face. He knew Adler was there, but ignored him right until he reached the station. He did manage to place his chart over the burn mark on the station table in time. It was best to avoid the embarrassment of his little mishap.

"I wanted to see for myself, so I took this little detour before work. You look happy," Adler started.

"It was just incredible. You should have seen it. Something was visible. I don't know what yet or where it came from, but matter just... appeared. Here, I will show you the video feed, but it's hard to see what my eyes did."

Noah projected the video onto a large screen. Next to it was a mass counter within the field.

"Watch as the test starts. On the right is the measurement of collective mass. Watch it shoot up. There, look."

"All I see is the area looks a little blue."

"That happens yes, and I hope to learn why. I'm thinking it could be because of the frequency that I'm using for resonance."

"There you go again. I have no idea what you are talking about."

Noah laughed mildly, "Right. Sorry. The important thing is that I got much, if not all, of what I need recorded, but even better, I get one more go at it just in case. And the amount of data I'm collecting each time would fill the average library."

"I saw you smiling, looking at it."

"Just at the possibilities. It's like when they discovered DNA and then began to sequence it. Once they did, it unlocked, and is still unlocking, a wealth of secrets. This is like the discovery and recording of DNA, and to decode it all will take time, and a lot of eyes. I will publish, but after I've had a little time to sort it all out, and after I catch up on some bills."

"Now you're talking. So, I should count you in on the consultation job for SciLab?"

"After this, yes, count me in."

"By the way, at the party Friday, the woman Nancy wants you to go out with was there. She's a geek, so your type, done up for this event, she looked drop dead gorgeous. I think you two would hit it off."

"Sure, any night after this part of the project is wrapped up, I'm game."

"I have to make a conference in Manhattan this morning so, I'll let you get back to your smiling. I'll touch base with you during the week, and I will see you here on Friday, well before 6:00 PM."

The Monday 5:30 PM ferry docked in Staten Island at the usual 5:55 and Sami walked his normal route down Bay Street and through the park. With the memory of last Friday flooding his mind, he wished he would see Amber again, but when he arrived at the park, the bench was empty. He sat there for a moment. If Stewart was right about spirits, seeing Amber then may have been only for him to confess how sorry he was that one time, and to tell her how much he loved her. He should have been grateful for that much, but he selfishly wanted to see her again.

Tuesday, when he returned, he did the same thing, sitting at that bench. He could not stay long, but there was almost an hour before Lis was off work at the book café and he would meet her for the packing she would do for him. After thirty minutes, Sami went to the apartment to drop off his laptop and straighten up even more so he didn't appear to be a complete slob. It was a noble effort, but given his lack of motivation recently, the place was still a bit cluttered. At 7:00, he went to get Lis as they had agreed.

As Sami approached the coffee shop Lis was already exiting and turned his way. He stopped and he let her walk over.

"Thanks for helping me with this, Lis."

Before she knew of Sami's loss, Lis had been bold in her flirting, but this time she was more reserved. Her eyes still lit up with a sweetness.

"Thank you for the opportunity to make some extra cash. I'm sorry for the reason, though."

"I appreciate the help. Amber always kept the apartment in shape, but her personal closet is in a state of disarray. I will show you, but, basically, I need to separate all her printed childhood photos and papers to give to her sister. The rest of it will go into storage for now."

As Sami opened the door to the apartment, it hit the pile of mail on the edge of the table that fell to the floor. His attempts to make the place look livable, still left it disheveled at best.

"You have to excuse the mess. I've just not been motivated."

Lis could feel the sadness in the apartment. Every pile around the room was stamped with the emotions Sami felt as he created them.

Lis's eyes glassed over and she looked deeply at Sami, "It's okay, Sami. I understand."

In that moment, she felt too much of Sami's hurt. He knew it, and glanced away to pick up the fallen mail. Lis walked in further and looked into the room. She continued to the end and peeked into the small kitchen. There were no dirty dishes or pots, but cabinets were open and items were left out on the counter. Sami noticed her spying the untidiness and followed her over.

"I don't yet know where all the items are. Amber always stocked the cabinets so…"

Sami picked up several of the boxes and Lis did as well. He showed her the closet in the bed room first and described the way he needed the contents to be sorted. It was the one on the right closet, closest to the window, medium sized, filled with clothes on the bar, a top shelf that went high crammed with items. The floor was overstuffed with assorted papers, small boxes, shoes and other items as well. Once that closet was done, he explained that the right closet in the entrance needed to be packed also, but in that closet was mostly just Amber's jackets. Sami reached into the top of his closet and pulled down a tape gun and sharpie.

"So, you have all you need. If you have any other questions just come see me, but don't worry too much if something makes it to the box for her sister Anne that shouldn't. She'll just send it back."

"I should be fine," Lis said, and touched Sami's hand softly.

He stared at her for just a moment, feeling a little awkward. At the same time, the touch felt welcome and comfortable.

Sami went into the living room to distract himself for a time. He put on the television low and moved a few items from the couch to the chair to sit down. Emotionally drained, he fell soundly asleep until he heard Lis shut his entrance door as she left. Groggy, he looked at his watch and it was almost 11:30 pm. He had been out that whole time and noticed that Lis had covered him in the small blanket from the bed. He saw a stack of boxes near the door, properly taped and labelled, but more than that, Lis had straightened up the living room all around him, and the kitchen too. There was a note on the coffee table.

*Sami*

*The bedroom closet is done and I will be back tomorrow to finish the entrance closet. I will meet you here at 7:05*

*Hugs,*
*Lis*

Noah was excited by all the data he had recorded. By that Wednesday, he had even been able to identify some of the particles, but all of which so far were aero microbiological in nature. But where had they come from, and where did they go when the field was removed? Given his second opportunity it helped him fine tune the instruments to look even deeper. And what was the faint blue glow? Maybe it was simply a byproduct of the resonant frequency he needed to use, but that was an answer he sought as well.

It was almost 5:30 pm when the elevator door opened and Adler stepped off. His voice echoed from that distance in this cavernous space.

"So, how is the work progressing?"

"Quite nicely, Adler. I've isolated and identified some of the particles. I need to monitor them on an even deeper microscopic level. While the field is on, aero microbiological, well, basically, microorganisms just appear."

"Huh?"

"Tiny life, Adler. Tiny airborne creatures."

"Now that's just weird," Adler laughed.

"The important part is that they are not there until the field is turned on and are gone when the test is over. I found my ghost particles."

"Still weird… So I came to give you a lift home, but how about first we stop for more of that pie?"

Noah laughed and powered down the station to ready the space to leave. Adler noticed the huge black burn mark on the station table this time and gave a smirk to Noah.

"Yup, almost toasted myself," Noah offered before Adler could say anything.

"Well, I'm glad you didn't. The insurance investigation paperwork alone would be mountainous," Adler said in a snarky tone, and patted his friend on the back.

They walked into a crowded café with only two small tables open closest to the back. Adler gawked at the cute young counter girl again until Noah smacked his arm, told him to go sit, and he would take care of it. She was relieved Noah had excused his friend and rewarded him with a slight smile. Noah prepared the coffees and carried them with the pie slices to the table on a tray. He placed the tray down to see Adler already in conversation with the owner, Stewart, who had politely asked him how things were going. Adler soon made an error in judgement.

"Well, it's going well. Noah here, has found his ghosts," Adler said with a small laugh.

"Adler, I'm glad you find it all funny. Funny guy. That's not exactly true, Stewart," Noah said.

It opened a window for Stewart and he offered a book to Noah which he politely set in front of him. It was a book on the study of metaphysics.

"Well, I had no idea that was what you were up to. I have a friend who found a ghost of his own," Stewart explained.

"That's not what Adler is joking about. I'm doing real science, and my findings are simply too new to adequately explain what is was that I have found. It will take time to even speculate, or let alone, have answers."

"Read that book. It may have the answers you are looking for."

Noah handed the book back to Stewart and thanked him, but told him no.

"I seriously appreciate it, Stewart, but I think I will try to discover the answers on my own," he said smiling.

"Suit yourself, but you should be more open minded. How do you explain the fact that my friend just talked with his recently deceased wife?"

"Is it a fact?"

"Well, I believe him. He's an honest guy and I do believe him. There are some things that cannot easily be explained."

"*That* we can agree on."

Lis finished up at 7 pm and made her way next door to Sami's apartment to finish her packing job. When he opened the door, he smiled this time.

"There's not much left for you to do. Can I make you a cup of coffee or tea?"

"Coffee would be nice, thanks."

"So just box all the jackets in there and I'll make us some coffee. I appreciate the way you cleaned up, and I'll pay you extra for that."

From the open kitchen entrance he could see Lis beginning to box up the contents of the closet. It did not take long before she got to the last one. It was a jacket in the back still in plastic and with the tag intact. Lis held it up and looked through the plastic to see a small black velvet jacket with a thin red stripe that ran up each sleeve. Sami could see her admiring it as he carried a tray to the coffee table.

"That one I bought for her, but she did not get a chance to wear it. It holds no real memories for me. Go ahead. Try it on."

Lis carefully removed the plastic, but left on the tag, and slipped on the jacket. It fit her perfectly and looked beautiful on her.

"Please keep it for helping me. It looks great on you and suits you."

Both of them sat on the couch and Sami poured the coffee into the cups and handed Lis the creamer and a spoon.

"Not sure I could say it suits me. I couldn't afford a jacket like this."

"It has nothing to do with money. If something suits you, it just does."

"Thanks Sami, you know I felt a little silly after flirting with you when we first met, and then learning you had just lost your wife. I'm sorry about that."

"Really, I hadn't noticed," Sami said, smiling.

"Seriously?" Lis asked, not realizing he was joking.

By Thursday, Sami was feeling good about things. Amber's items were packed and recent possessions would soon be stored and the remaining items brought to her sister, Anne. On his way home this time, he passed the bench and continued through the park to home. That was a milestone in recovery. The next day, with his life sorted and apartment in order, it gave him a new outlook. He could now just look ahead.

Noah was cataloging some of the organisms when he heard the elevator door open and saw Adler arriving as he said he would. He was here to see the second and final opening of the field. It was almost 4:00 in the afternoon and well in time.

"I told you I'd join you for this one."

"Wait until you see it, Adler. It looks amazing just to witness, but then to recognize what you are seeing, even better."

"Well, you might recognize it, but I sure as hell won't," he said, laughing.

"Essentially, the normal microorganisms in the air can be kicked up by wind off the soil, but as humans cough, sneeze, and talk, they also discharge living organisms into the air. It's not their natural habitat given scarce moisture, but they live for some time. There are living things evident before the field is activated, but when the field is turned on it is a substantial increase in mass. From microscopic recordings, additional lifeforms appear from seemingly nowhere."

"And that means?"

"I don't yet know, but hope to find out. The matter must come from somewhere. Taken simply; matter is energy. The first law of thermodynamics means that in a closed system, the total amount of energy is fixed, although it can change form. I just need to find that somewhere, and there are seemingly layers of new matter."

The boat docked and lowered its ramp at a normal time 5:54 and Sami headed down Bay Street toward home. He reached the bench just before 6:00 and sat for a moment. No one was around, except for that old woman sitting on a bench a distance away. Today, she looked sad again, but at least she was not crying.

Noah received a call from Captain Lambertson that the power would be coming on, moments late. He assured him he would have the 30 minutes, but Noah was happy with the time he could get anyway. Adler sat and waited with him and then the meters registered power was live on the wire at 6:01. Noah stood up and walked to the panel. He pressed to engage the sequence. The two of them watched as the rotations occurred in the towers until the order locked into place, then they could hear the burst from the capacitors, and the surge of power. The sound settled into the choir of soft whispers. Adler was captivated for a moment by the sounds, and the glow of blue in the field so he walked closer for a better look. When he finally turned back, Noah had vanished.

It was just about 6:01 pm when Sami had a sinking feeling seeing a faint blue haze envelope the area again. He saw the woman's little dog run from the bushes and jump on her lap as she smiled again. At that same moment, from the corner of his eye he saw Amber sitting next to him again on the bench. This time, when she noticed him, she looked frightened. There was no time to reach for her again before she quickly stood up and backed away.

"Who are you and where did you come from?" Amber asked.

"It's me, Amber. It's Sami," he said, standing up.

Visibly shaken she backed away even further.

"You are not my Sami. Like now, last time you were wearing black, but when we left the park you vanished in front of me. My Sami was looking for me and he was wearing a blue shirt. I made the mistake of talking about our conversation and now Sami believes I've totally lost my mind. And now I am really thinking maybe I have. So now he really does plan to leave me and it's your fault."

"I'm so sorry, Amber. I don't understand how this is happening. There was something I never told you last time because I didn't want to frighten you, but you died. I was so happy to see you last week because I thought I had you back."

"I'm not dead. Maybe crazy, but not dead. And you certainly don't act like my Sami."

"It took losing you to wake me up, Amber. I don't know what had gotten into me, but when I lost you, I realized that I couldn't live without you. Now, it seems I just made it worse for you by not being honest last week. I'm sorry."

She could feel his sincerity and it calmed her just enough to stay.

"This is just crazy. I believe you when you say you are just as in the dark as I am about who we both are to each other, but I'm quite sure you don't want to hurt me. You know just how he thinks. What am I going to do about this? How can I make my Sami love me again?"

Noah found himself in an empty space with all his equipment broken down, packed and stacked in a row for a pickup. On top of one of the cases was the bottle of wine he had bought last week, but unopened. The only thing he could see was that the room still had the faint blue glow. So many things went through his head, like whether he was pushed ahead in time among others, and then he heard the elevator coming up. When the door opened, he saw Adler, stunned at the sight of him.

"You disappeared in front of me, Adler. We were in the middle of the second run. Where did you go, and why is my equipment packed up?" Noah asked.

"What the hell? How did you do this? There was never a second run, Noah. You were killed on the night of the first. I spoke at your funeral, and I saw you buried."

"I'm quite alive thank you. Is this a joke, old friend?"

"I'm dead serious. The trucks need to load out off hours so I am here to let them in shortly to retrieve your things. The capacitors were hauled off during the week and they are already back at SciLab."

Noah then knew he was serious, and he pulled out one of the rolling cases and frantically started to open it.

"What are you doing?" Adler asked.

"I want to make sure the data is still there, that I captured from the first night."

Amber grew more comfortable with this Sami even though she knew he was not hers. Sami grew almost jealous that there was another, from her point of view and then angry that her Sami was about to make the mistake of his life. If only he realized what this Sami was now so certain of.

Amber noticed a small smile on Sami's face and asked, "What?"

Sami snapped back from a thought and realized what he was feeling.

"I accept now that you are not her, but it does give me a sense of peace to know that somewhere you are okay. Amber is okay."

With a twisted side look, Amber with tears in her eyes, seemed ever more distraught.

"I'm sorry you lost her, Sami. I really am. I see how much you loved her. I only wish my Sami felt that way about me."

At first they both sat in their places on the bench, Amber still crying. Then she felt completely relaxed and she buried her head in his chest.

"I don't want my Sami to leave me. He thinks I've completely lost my mind, and I knew I was getting better. Now you came along."

"I am sorry, Amber, but you're right. I don't know how this happened, but I know what's in my heart, and I love you. I mean my Amber. We need to stop your Sami from making a huge mistake. He simply has no idea what he could be throwing away."

Noah only needed to power on the main console and data mining systems to see if the data was still there, and after some time he powered it all up and it was.

"So glad it's still here," he told Adler.

"I thought you might be a little more concerned with the fact that I told you I saw you buried, you know, that you're dead."

"Okay, then how did I die?"

"They determined that when you switched the feed to the capacitor bank last week while wrapping up, the cover blew off and it arced. It struck you, and killed you instantly."

"That missed me. Not by much, but it did. Promise me, though, if something happens to me, please turn over the data to Dr. Greene. I owe him one."

"You got it, but you cheated death. What can happen to you worse? It's almost 6:30 and I'll need to let in the movers. Don't go anywhere, okay? Better yet, come down with me."

Sami was still hugging Amber, trying to think of anything he could do.

"Amber, you remember how much my grandfather adored you. I was so glad he got to know you. Just before he passed away, I had talked with him about us. He told me that from the moment he met you, he knew you were the one I was meant to be with. He understood about your anxiety and told me how beyond it was the gentlest of troubled souls."

"So, I should tell this to my Sami?"

"Tell him this," he said and whispered something into Amber's ear just before she disappeared.

Sami could see the old woman on the bench across and he saw her dog vanish from her lap. Her face turned sad again, but this time he walked over and crouched down looking up at her.

"But isn't it good to know they are doing okay somewhere?" he asked.

She looked down at Sami and smiled.

"Yes, young man. Yes, it is. Was that your girlfriend with you?"

"So you saw her too? She was my wife who recently died."

"Critter, my dog, died a month ago. He was my only companion. I was lost without him. I guess this was a gift to help us move on."

"Perhaps it was," Sami said and reached out to take the woman's hand.

"I'm sorry about your wife. She was very beautiful."

"Yes, she was. I'm sorry for you too, but happy we had this chance."

They would both later learn it was to be their last chance.


Adler heard the power feed shut down and saw his friend Noah reappear in front of him. The sequence ending brought him back into the room.

"That was some trick, Noah," Adler said almost angrily.

"You don't know the half of it."

"I didn't know how to stop this thing. You scared the shit out of me. Where the hell did you go?"

"I have some ideas, but I can't say for sure. But what I can say definitively is that there's more to my field than I originally thought."

"Yeah, you can say that."

Noah checked the data he had collected and initiated a remote backup before powering down the remaining gear. Adler was repeatedly asking where Noah went, but he was ignored until all the tasks were finally completed.

"Well, I will tell you what I know, good friend, but first you need to promise not to have me committed. Oh, and the first order of business is that you promise never to let me make my own electrical feed connections in the future."

Sami crossed the park and saw Lis standing outside the coffee shop wearing the black jacket he gave her. She noticed he was coming, but waited for him to come close before she spun herself around.

"Nice, huh? You have good taste, Sami."

"Well, it looks great on you. I thought you didn't work Fridays."

"I don't. I was just stopping by. I plan to meet up with friends and go dancing."

She felt like flirting again and beamed the sweetest look.

"Would you like to come?"

She could see something had changed in Sami. He seemed more content, more settled.

"Not tonight, but you'll invite me again?"

"Yes, of course. Hey, I have a little time before I leave. Would you like to have a cup of coffee?"

"In there?" Sami asked, pointing at the coffee shop.

"No, in your apartment if you don't mind. I'm in the café quite enough," Lis laughed.

Amber quietly opened the door to their apartment and saw Sami sitting on the couch with the deepest look of worry. He looked up almost in tears.

"Where did you go again? I looked for you where you wait for me, but you never showed up."

Amber started to cry and she tried to hold Sami, but he held her away.

"I did show up. It was you who had changed."

"I love you, Amber, but recently your actions have been more than I can take, and this story of another me. My heart is breaking, but I can't help you."

"But I realized it was not you. Something happened to me, Sami. I don't know what, but I am trying the best I can. Do you remember how much your grandfather loved me as his own? Just weeks before he died you told him you were not sure about me. You spoke with him about us"

"Who told you that?"

"Your grandfather told you he knew we were meant to be together from the moment he met me."

"Yes, he said that. I've never told that to anyone."

"He also gave you advice. He said I was a beautiful bird with a broken wing. He said, help me and I'll fly, but never away."

Tears came to Sami's eyes, stunned, he asked nothing more. His grandfather had reached from beyond and woken his empathy, and deepest love for Amber again. He held his wife tightly, repeatedly kissing her head, telling her he loved her and was never letting go.

# TWO ESSAYS

Dear God - an essay by Ray Melnik

*Twelve-year-old, Jimmy Taylor washed up for bed after a birthday that came with no cake, no candles and no presents. But there was still a smile as he looked into the small round mirror resting on the sink. Before getting into bed, he looked up.*

"God; I know you are really busy, but I hope you're listening. Dad's unemployment ran out and Mom says she doesn't know what we're going to do. We're already behind on all the bills. You know it's been hard since Jenny got sick and Mom worries that something will happen to Jenny if we can't control her diabetes. There hasn't been enough money to pay for health care since Dad was laid off. The city gives Jenny care for free now, but Mom and she spend hours waiting. Mom did say she was grateful that it at least covers the insulin. Dad looks for work every day, but Mom can't go back until we get Jenny stable.

"I understand why you didn't help me the other times I've asked. You can't grant every prayer. But I really need you this time, God. Mom and Dad are putting all our things in boxes right now. There are too many months of unpaid rent due with nothing to pay it with. They won't say where we are going. I don't think they even know yet. Please, God, I don't want to move again.

"But what hurts the most is that Mom and Dad were arguing. Dad got angrier than I had even seen him and even raised his hand to Mom. He stopped himself and never touched her, though. I went to Mom when she was in her room crying and she told me that Dad is a good man. She said that all he ever wanted was to be able to care for his family. But when he lost his job he lost his dignity, she said.

"So you can understand why I need your help so badly. I know you've been around. Marylyn, the deli owner's daughter, told me you answered her prayers when you gave her beautiful weather for her wedding last weekend. And Billy Barnes told me his whole team prayed to win the

Little League regional championship this past week and you blessed them with the prize.

"So if you are still around and listening, please know that we have always believed in you. Mom and Dad say you have a plan for us and we should never question your judgment.

"But please, God. If your plans don't include a job for my Dad soon, would you please consider changing them? I'm asking for him. I can do without the other things I've been praying for. My wheelchair still has a few more years of life in it."

Dear Humans - an essay by Ray Melnik

We heard there would be a message, days before it happened. The social media sites were suddenly and simultaneously flooded with the announcement about it, in every language. It never referred to their dominant deity, but simply that it would be a message from the creator. Most of us considered it a hoax, but some religious groups became increasingly nervous. What if it was the creator? It might just reveal if they had chosen the correct path over all the others.

To the scientists and skeptics, it was a field day as they frantically searched for the source of the announcement. To them it was a game trying to reveal the trickster. By the time the message was due to come they had not succeeded in locating a single source, but found it came from absolutely everywhere. Given all the worldwide broadcast and media security measures in place it was something experts considered impossible.

I was walking up Broadway through Times Square when all the giant screens on the buildings began showing the most relevant and violent scenes throughout history. Everyone stopped and watched when they began to realize this must be the mysterious message from the one who claimed to be the creator. When we looked at our phones they were all showing these same scenes. We would later find out that this was broadcast to every screen on the planet. What we were seeing in the historic footage was horrific and graphic. Much of it would later be determined to be accurate, but from no known existing source or archives.

Then the scenes changed to the best of humanity, with examples of selfless acts of bravery and charity. There were the sciences in the pursuits of discovery and the development of life saving cures. That soon changed to a frame with thousands of depictions of human deities. The screen continued to loop and we heard the voice for the first time. It was the voice of a woman, and later it was revealed that we were hearing her in our own languages no matter where we were in the world.

*"Island Earth. When I set in motion all the natural processes that led to you I had no intention of intervening or interfering. All of the necessary tools have always been at your fingertips and my intention was to allow nature to take its course. This is true as well for the endless worlds stretched across the cosmos, where beings just like you search for their own meaning. There are those at your stage, some have come and gone and others are just being born.*

*So why speak with you now? I've watched your wars, your hate, your killing and your evil. I have seen how cruel you can be to one another and how easily swayed many of you have been throughout your history. There are those of you so greedy that you would pull the bread from the mouth of a poor child and ignore the aftermath while living deeply buried within your wealth. There are many others who allow this to continue unchecked. But I have also witnessed acts of selflessness and compassion, kindness and generosity.*

*To all the religions: You are all a little right, but all a bit wrong. You cannot pray to help others. You must help others. Nature will create problems that I have never interfered with. I look for no worship and I am none of the gods you have been told I was. I also see the good you have provided, as a voice for the poor, your food drives, and your contributions. This is a good thing.*

*Atheists and skeptics: You had it right about all the world's religions, but you were wrong about me. Still I see that most of you hold goodness in your hearts no different than any believer. No doubt you will dispute this is me and look for proof. That is a good thing.*

*So my intention is not to tell you what might come for you, but simply to say that you are at a precipice. I have no chosen people. You all matter, each and every one of you. I do not cause illness; natural processes do, but you have brilliant minds and can find cures and ways to ease pain. That also goes for maintaining the health of your planet. You will get no others with this much potential. And all these boundaries you created will never mask the fact that you are all related. And who you love, that's always up to you. No love is bad.*

*So before I leave you on your own again I will only ask that you choose wisely. Only you can make a difference in each other's lives."*

That would be the last time we heard her voice.

CPSIA information can be obtained at www.ICGtesting.com
Printed in the USA
BVOW08s2222030516

446622BV00001B/2/P